It Starts With a Raindrop

words&pictures

© 2024 Quarto Publishing Group USA Inc.

Words by Aimee Gallagher
Illustrations by Sally Garland

Editor: Helen Mortimer
Art Director: Susi Martin
Associate Publisher: Holly Willsher

This edition published in 2024 by words & pictures,
an imprint of The Quarto Group.
100 Cummings Center,
Suite 265D Beverly,
MA 01915, USA.
T (978) 282-9590 F (978) 283-2742
www.quarto.com

A CIP record for this book is available from the Library of Congress.

ISBN: 978-0-7112-8594-1

9 8 7 6 5 4 3 2 1

Manufactured in Guangdong, China CC042024

It Starts With a Raindrop

Illustrations by Sally Garland

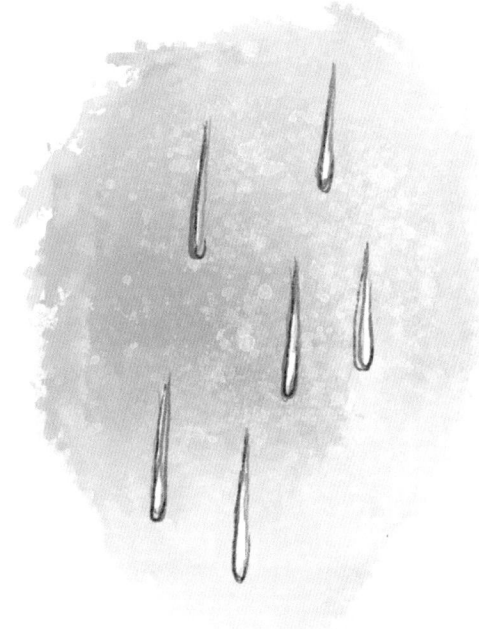

It starts with a raindrop. . .

but where does it land?

A splash in a puddle?

A mark on the sand?

Wherever rain falls,
it drenches the earth—
turning it into
a place of rebirth.

In cold places
rain comes in flurries of snow
or terrible blizzards
when icy winds blow.

And where it is hotter
the rain can feel warm,
as it falls from the sky
in a tropical storm.

The rain soaks the ground
where plants and trees grow,
and fills up the rivers
where animals go.

From the wide ocean blue
to the tiniest stream,
the sun warms the water
and turns it to steam.

The steam rises up
floating high in the air,
then some of it cools
making clouds here and there.

Clouds are collections
of droplets of rain,
just waiting to fall
all over again!

And if there's a shower
with the sun shining through,
a rainbow might form
for a minute or two.

Water is precious—
it keeps us alive.
Its cycle makes sure
that our planet will thrive.

So put on your rain boots